TO MY SON, SANDES.

# BORN FROM THE HEART

BY
BERTA SERRANO

ILLUSTRATIONS BY
ALFONSO SERRANO

STERLING CHILDREN'S BOOKS
New York

Rose always knew she wanted to be a mom.

Every day, she dreamed of having a family of her own.

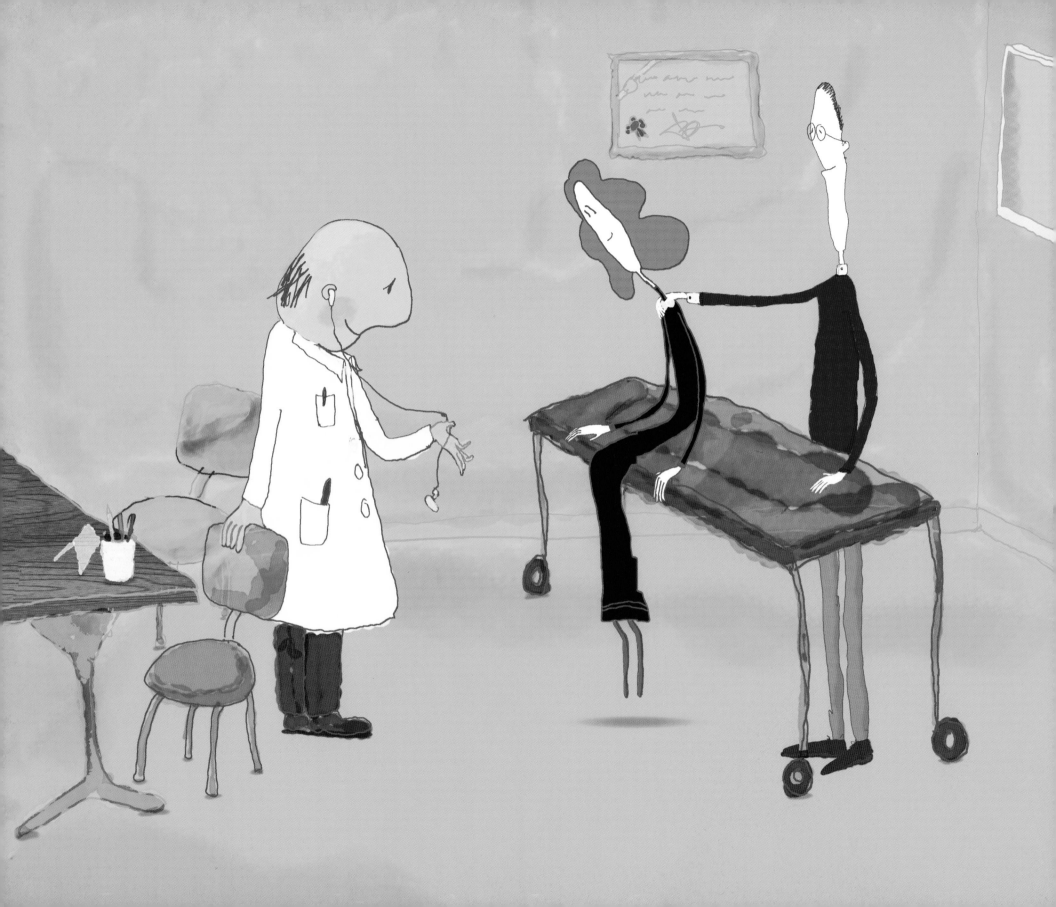

One morning, Rose and her husband, Charlie, went to the doctor to learn how they might get started.

The doctor, who was a very wise man, gave them a magic recipe for how to become parents. They had to mix:

- 1 pound of love
- 2 cups of enthusiasm
- 1½ tablespoons of patience

And so it was . . .
Rose and Charlie were ready to give it their best try.

That evening, they prepared the magic recipe. When Rose took two spoonfuls of the potion, the effect was almost instantaneous. She felt something new beating inside her chest.

"Come over here, Charlie!" Rose said. "You have to listen to this!"

"What is happening to you?" asked Charlie.

The next day, Rose and Charlie went to see the doctor again.

"This is amazing!" said the doctor. "I believe you are going to have a child. I can see something gleaming in your heart!"

This was the most extraordinary news in the world.
Rose and Charlie were so happy, they jumped for joy.

Every day, Rose's heart grew bigger and bigger.

From the very first heartbeat, Rose loved her
baby to the moon and back.

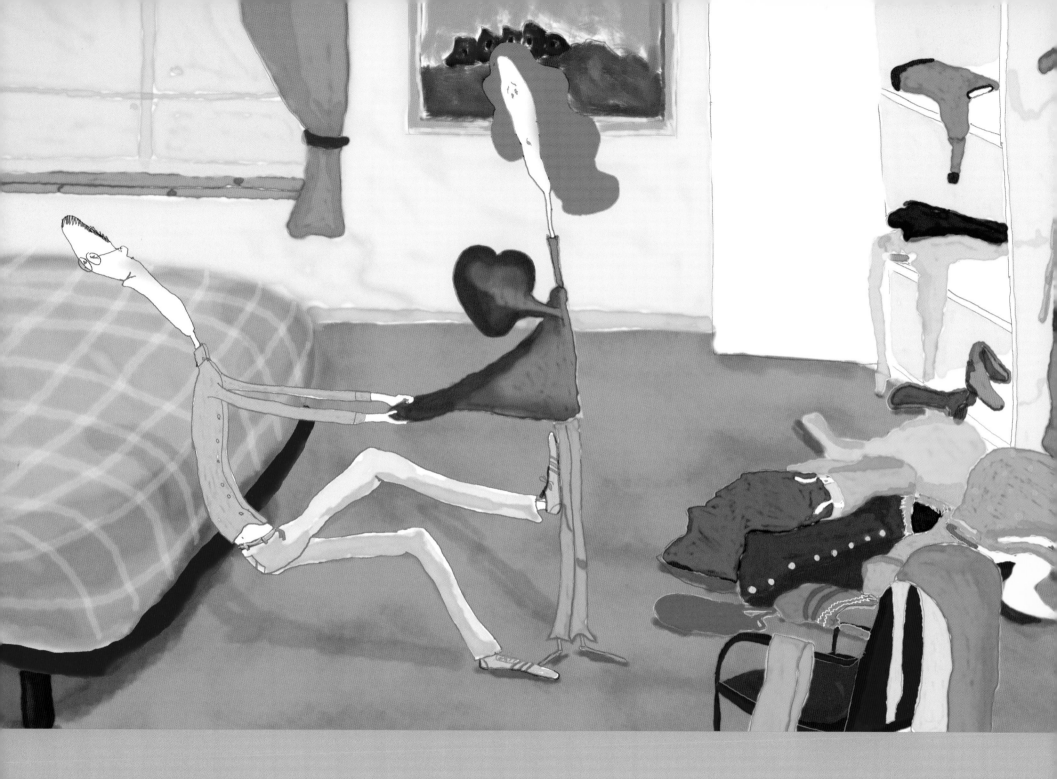

It was not long before Rose had trouble fitting into her clothes. Her heart would just not stop growing!

And just like that . . .
she found a special store for special moms like her.

Rose dreamed of her baby every night. She imagined a sweet little face and a loving smile. She couldn't wait to share hugs and giggles.

During the day, Rose and Charlie prepared a lovely room for their baby. It had a tiny little bed with a cozy blanket and all kinds of fun toys to play with, and books for them to read together.

One day, the phone rang. It was time!
Rose and Charlie had to get ready for the greatest trip of their lives.

Their plane flew over marshmallow clouds.

They crossed landscapes of every imaginable color . . .

and climbed up and down never-ending mountains.

Rose and Charlie arrived at a little house in the middle
of a green valley.

The door of the house opened.

Suddenly, something magical happened. It was Rose's heart again! She felt an extraordinary burst of happiness—a rainbow of colors, laughter, and the most wonderful sounds.

And then Rose saw her baby for the first time. She ran and embraced her little one with all of her love, just as she had done in her dreams.

She squeezed her baby as tightly as she could and kissed the beautiful face one hundred million times.

This is how Rose's baby was born—from her heart.

## AUTHOR'S NOTE

When my husband, Carlos, and I met our son for the first time, he was a fragile three-and-a-half-year-old boy. His caretaker at the orphanage had told him that we were his new parents, and that he would go away with us to start a new life. He was frightened when we met and deeply sad to leave everything he knew and loved behind. Nonetheless, he endured this extreme transition with a unique resilience.

Once we arrived home with our son, we welcomed his past and deliberately made it part of our present. We encouraged his questions and answered them as honestly as we could. We were going to build our family on the grounds of trust and love.

It was not until one random morning at the doctor's office two years after his arrival that something clicked in my son's mind. Although we had spoken about it before, he realized for the first time that he was not my biological child.

His discovery opened in him an emotional void, and with it came great distress and grief. As a mom, I wanted an immediate solution, the magical action that would forever take his pain away. But all I could really do was embrace him, contain his pain with my love, and be present to talk about anything he wanted.

It was this very event that inspired the book *Born From the Heart*.

My wish as a mom is to empower my son to embrace his life in full and without fears, feeling loved, secure, and aware. With this story, I wanted to create a playful scenario for us to celebrate the birth of our family, and to give our love for each other a renewed light.

STERLING CHILDREN'S BOOKS
New York
An Imprint of Sterling Publishing
387 Park Avenue South
New York, NY 10016

STERLING CHILDREN'S BOOKS and the distinctive Sterling Children's Books
logo are trademarks of Sterling Publishing Co., Inc.

© 2013 by Berta Serrano Vreugde
Illustrations © 2013 by Alfonso Serrano Vreugde

ISBN 978-1-4549-1144-9

Library of Congress Cataloging-in-Publication Data available.

Distributed in Canada by Sterling Publishing
c/o Canadian Manda Group, 165 Dufferin Street
Toronto, Ontario, Canada M6K 3H6
Distributed in the United Kingdom by GMC Distribution Services
Castle Place, 166 High Street, Lewes, East Sussex, England BN7 1XU
Distributed in Australia by Capricorn Link (Australia) Pty. Ltd.
P.O. Box 704, Windsor, NSW 2756, Australia

For information about custom editions, special sales, and premium and corporate purchases,
please contact Sterling Special Sales at 800-805-5489 or specialsales@sterlingpublishing.com.

Printed in Canada
Lot #:
2  4  6  8  10  9  7  5  3  1
08/13

www.sterlingpublishing.com/kids